MAGNUS
AND THE
NIGHT LION

Sanne Dufft

Floris

Magnus had a hat and a sword.

   With his hat and sword he was big and strong, bold and fearless.

"I am a knight with a shining sword. Fight me if you dare!"
he shouted.

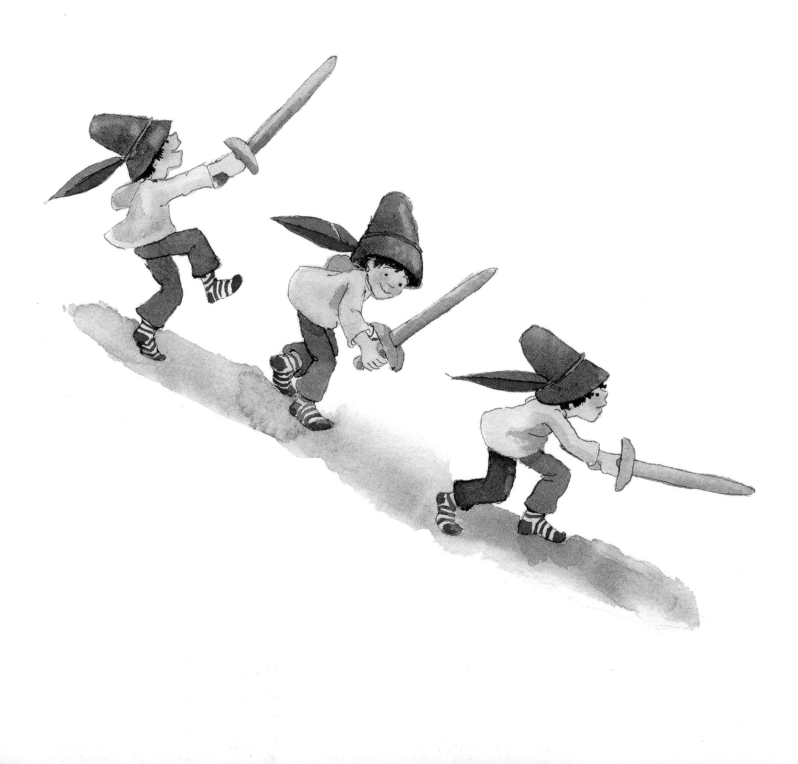

But his little sister didn't like fighting,
and Mama said she was too busy.

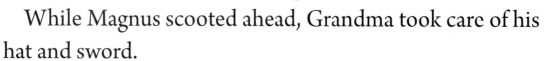

Grandma said, "Magnus, how about you come for a walk in the forest with me? Brave knights need lots of fresh air."

While Magnus scooted ahead, Grandma took care of his hat and sword.

They look quite good on her, thought Magnus.

That night, Magnus dreamed of the forest. It was dark.

The Shadowman in the forest wanted to steal his hat and sword.

Magnus woke, frightened.
Mama came and hugged him.
"The Shadowman isn't real," she said.
The hug helped. A little.

At bedtime, Magnus curled up holding
his lion close, and fell asleep.

"The Shadowman *is* real," Magnus told her. "He's much bigger than me. He wants my hat and my sword."

"Don't worry, darling. He isn't here when you wake up."

But what did Mama know? It wasn't *her* dream.

The next day, when Grandma came, she brought a lion for Magnus.

That's funny, thought Magnus. *It's not my birthday.*

"Everyone needs a lion sometimes," said Grandma. "Especially in the dark."

Magnus said, "I love lions."

"They're a lot of work," warned Grandma. "A lion needs a cave to rest in and a knight to be its best friend."

"And mountains of food!" said Magnus.

"That's right," said Grandma. "When lions are hungry, they roar terribly."

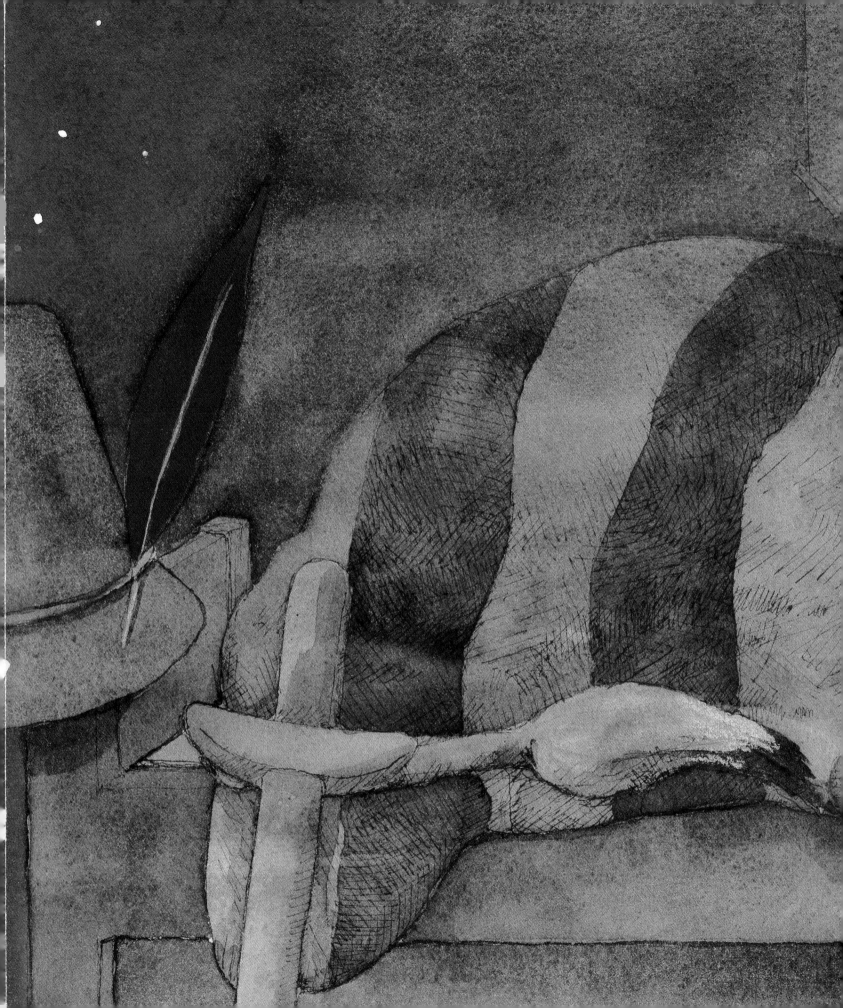

Suddenly there was a noise: sticks cracked nearby.

"Do you hear that?" Magnus whispered. "The Shadowman is coming."

"Hold on, scaredy-cat," said his Night Lion, "you're a brave knight, remember? Put on your hat, grab your sword and climb on my back."

The Night Lion roared, oh how loudly he roared! He charged through the forest, straight towards the Shadowman!

"I am a knight with a shining sword. Fight me if you dare!" shouted Magnus.
He was big and strong, bold and fearless.

"What's all this crashing around?" asked Papa.
"Don't worry!" said Magnus. "Tell Mama
we've chased the Shadowman away! You can go
back to sleep now."

Magnus had a hat and a sword. With his hat and sword he was
big and strong, bold and fearless.

And now he had a lion too.
Together, Magnus and his Night Lion were mighty. Especially in the dark.